A GOLDEN BOOK • NEW YORK

Special thanks to Vicki Jaeger, Monica Okazaki, Ann McNeill, Emily Kelly, Sharon Woloszyk, Julia Phelps, Tanya Mann, Rob Hudnut, David Wiebe, Shelley Dvi-Vardhana, Michelle Cogan, Rainmaker Entertainment, Walter P. Martishius, Carla Alford, Rita Lichtwardt, Kathy Berry, and Miranda Nolte

www.randomhouse.com/kids
ISBN: 978-0-375-87186-3
Printed in the United States of America
10 9 8 7 6 5 4 3 2 1

Adapted by Kristen Depken

Based on the screenplay by Elise Allen

Illustrated by Ulkutay Design Group

*E*very year, the kingdom of Gardania celebrated the opening day of Princess Charm School with a grand procession. Girls born into royalty came to the palace from far and wide, eager to enroll as princesses-in-training. And each year, one lucky girl was chosen to attend Princess Charm School as a future Lady Royal, a princess's most trusted advisor.

In a small apartment on the outskirts of Gardania, a young woman named Blair lived with her foster mom and her little sister, Emily. All Emily ever dreamed about was becoming a princess. Blair loved Emily's imagination and encouraged her to believe in her dreams.

One afternoon, Blair arrived home from work to find Emily watching the Princess Charm School procession on television.

The school's headmistress, Madame Privet, read the name of the winner of the Lady Royal contest: "Blair Willows."

Emily had entered Blair in the contest without her knowing!

Before Blair knew what was happening, a palace guard was at the door.

"I'm here to take you to Princess Charm School," he told her.

"There's been a mistake," Blair said. "I don't belong with a bunch of princesses. And I have responsibilities here."

But Blair knew that if she became a Lady Royal, she could help her family. She finally agreed to accompany the guard to her new school.

The guard took Blair to a beautiful castle. "This can't be real," she said. As she approached the entrance, a big, friendly golden retriever came running out to greet her. He wagged his tail excitedly and licked Blair's face as she pet him.

"Prince," she read on his name tag. "Good boy."

Headmistress Privet welcomed Blair and showed her around the school. Then she gave Blair a uniform and introduced her to Grace, Blair's new sprite. Blair couldn't believe how amazing it all was. She even had a sparkly, jeweled locker!

Soon Blair met Isla and Hadley, two princesses-in-training—and her roommates. They all became friends right away.

Blair quickly realized that becoming a Lady Royal would be hard work. She had to walk, talk, and act like a princess—even though she really didn't feel like one!

Blair's first class was taught by Dame Devin, a mean instructor. Dame Devin explained that years ago, Queen Isabella of Gardania and her family had died in a terrible accident. Dame Devin's daughter, Delancy, was next in line for the throne. But Isla and Hadley told Blair there were rumors that Queen Isabella's baby daughter, Sophia, had survived!

Blair tried not to let snooty Dame Devin and Delancy bother her. She worked hard, and with Headmistress Privet's help, her royal skills soon began to improve.

One day, Headmistress Privet invited a group of princes to dance class. Delancy wanted the handsome Prince Nicholas to be her partner—but he was paired with Blair instead. The two only had eyes for each other.

"You dance beautifully," Prince Nicholas told Blair.

Delancy, who overheard, was furious.

That evening, Dame Devin was hosting a manners class and dinner at the Palace of Gardania. As part of their preparation, Blair, Hadley, and Isla spent the afternoon at the spa.

While their personal sprites did their nails, the girls chatted. "I'd love to find out more about what happened to Queen Isabella and the lost Princess Sophia," said Isla.

"I want to find out more about Gardania's Magical Crown," said Hadley. "They say that the crown glows when it's placed on the head of the true heir of Gardania."

"The earlier we get to the palace, the more we will see!" said Blair.

When Blair, Hadley, and Isla got back to their room, they gasped. Their uniforms had been torn to shreds!

"It was Delancy," said Hadley. "It had to be." Blair and Isla agreed.

"What are we going to do?" asked Isla. "We're not allowed in class without our uniforms."

Blair had an idea. She picked up the shredded uniforms. "They just need a little alteration," she said with a smile.

With the help of their sprites, Blair, Hadley, and Isla got to work.

Meanwhile, at the palace, Dame Devin looked at her
watch. "Blair, Hadley, and Isla are running late," she said.
"I'm afraid we'll have to fail all three of them."

Just as Dame Devin was about to close the palace doors,
Blair and her friends came rushing in.

"Those aren't school-issued uniforms!" cried Dame Devin.

"They are made entirely from the material in our original uniforms," replied Blair. "We've just arranged things a little differently."

"And beautifully, at that," declared Headmistress Privet approvingly. "Come join the class."

As the girls took their seats, Dame Devin pulled Delancy aside. "I need you to find some dirt on Blair Willows—something we can use to get her expelled."

Headmistress Privet gave the girls time to explore the palace before dinner. Blair, Hadley, and Isla headed down a grand hallway.

Suddenly, Isla pointed to a portrait hanging on the wall. "It's a picture of Blair!" she cried.

Blair took a step closer and read the nameplate: " 'Princess Isabella, age eighteen.' " Blair looked exactly like the young queen!

"Blair, didn't you tell us that your foster mom found you on her doorstep?" asked Isla.

"Yes," said Blair, "about seventeen years ago."

"You could be Princess Sophia!" said Hadley.

Suddenly, the dinner bell rang. As the girls headed back to the main hall, Delancy stepped out of the shadows. She had heard the girls' conversation. Delancy stared at the portrait, wondering whether she was really the rightful heir to Gardania after all.

While the class sat down to dinner, Dame Devin made an announcement: Delancy's first act as princess would be to tear down all the buildings in the poorer sections of Gardania, to create parks and preserve the beauty of the kingdom.

"But my home is there!" cried Blair.

"If I were you, I'd leave this school immediately and get my family ready to move," said Dame Devin.

Blair knew she had to stop Delancy and Dame Devin. And she was beginning to think that maybe she really was Princess Sophia. But there was only one way to prove it.

"Gardania's Magical Crown!" Hadley said. "It must be in the palace."

The girls vowed to find it before Coronation Day.

Meanwhile, Dame Devin was more determined than ever to have Blair thrown out of Princess Charm School. That evening, she staged a fire drill. While Blair, Hadley, and Isla were outside, Dame Devin hid a necklace in their room.

When the girls returned to their room, Dame Devin stormed in with Headmistress Privet and a palace guard.

"I'm sure it's some kind of mistake," insisted Headmistress Privet. "But Dame Devin believes you stole her jewelry."

"We didn't steal anything!" cried Isla.

But when the guard searched the room, he found the hidden necklace. Headmistress Privet had no choice—she ordered the girls to be locked up until after the coronation.

The security guard led Blair, Hadley, and Isla down the hallway.

"Stop!" Delancy ordered the guard. "I've got something else in mind for the prisoners. You may turn them over to me."

When they were alone, Delancy said to Blair, "Are you really Princess Sophia?" she asked.

"I don't know for sure," replied Blair. "But I think so."

"I think so, too," said Delancy. She had had enough of her mother's lies. She handed Blair a map of the palace. "There's something of yours inside the vault."

"Gardania's Magical Crown?" asked Blair.

Delancy nodded. "You have to find it before I am crowned at the coronation," she said. "Now go!"

Blair, Hadley, and Isla hurried to the palace. Using a rope, they scaled the outer wall and climbed through an open window.

Once inside the palace, the girls made their way to the basement vault.

"Please enter your password," came a voice from the security keypad. Blair, Hadley, and Isla tried several different codes, but none of them worked.

Then Blair had an idea. "The day my mom found me!" she said. She entered the date into the keypad, and the door to the vault swung open.

"Look!" cried Blair. Gardania's Magical Crown rested
inside the vault.

Just as Blair reached for it, Dame Devin appeared with two
guards. The mean teacher grabbed the crown off its pedestal.
"You'll never be more than a poor contest girl."

Dame Devin slammed the door shut and reset the
password. Blair, Hadley, and Isla were locked in the vault!

Luckily, Isla remembered the tune of the numbers that Dame Devin had typed into the keypad.

Hadley broke open the keypad, and Blair hooked her phone up to it. Then Isla played the tune on the phone.

The vault door opened!

Blair, Hadley, and Isla raced out just as the coronation was beginning.

On the palace stage, Dame Devin watched impatiently as Delancy did everything she could to delay her coronation.

"Now everyone must pat her head and rub her stomach at the same time," Delancy told the audience.

"Enough!" shouted Dame Devin. "Crown her!"

Suddenly, Blair burst into the hall. "Wait!" she cried.

"I am making a claim to the throne," Blair declared as she climbed onto the stage. "I am Princess Sophia, daughter of Queen Isabella!"

Dame Devin tried to grab the Magical Crown of Gardania, but Blair's, Hadley's, and Isla's sprites got to it first. They quickly placed the crown on Blair's head.

The crown immediately began to glow brightly, and Blair's outfit magically transformed into a long, glittering gown. Blair truly *was* Princess Sophia, the rightful heir to the throne of Gardania!

"Do you have any idea what you've done?" Dame Devin shouted at Delancy. "I eliminated Queen Isabella so *you* could be princess one day!"

The coronation was being broadcast on live television throughout the entire kingdom—and Dame Devin had just confessed to her crime. A palace guard quickly came forward and took her away.

Blair was overwhelmed as her new subjects rose to honor her. "Thank you," she said. "I promise to work hard and always live up to my princess potential."

"Blair, it is customary for the Princess of Gardania to choose her Lady Royal after her coronation," said Headmistress Privet.

"It would be an incredible privilege to have as my Lady Royal . . . Delancy," Blair announced.

Delancy was shocked.

"I wouldn't be wearing this crown without your help," said Blair. "Will you accept?"

"I would be honored . . . Your Highness," replied Delancy, and she bowed.

The crowd burst into applause.

After the coronation ceremony, there was a big party to celebrate. Blair was dancing with her friends when Prince Nicholas approached her.

"Congratulations, Princess Blair . . . or Sophia. What do I call you?" he asked bashfully.

"You can call me Blair," Blair replied. "Congratulations on your coronation, too."

"Wouldst thou do me the honor of a dance?" asked Nicholas.

Blair smiled and took his hand. "I would be most delighted."

Suddenly Blair was told that she had two very special visitors.

"Emily! Mom!" Blair rushed to her family and wrapped them in a huge hug. "Welcome to our new home!" she told them, gesturing to the palace.

"If you're a princess now, does that mean I'm a princess, too?" asked Emily. Blair smiled at her sister, then placed Gardania's Magical Crown on her head.

"Of course! There's a princess in every girl!" Blair said with a twinkle in her eye.

Then Blair led her family into the palace to start their new life.

the
End